Firefighter Mary

by Ami Shipp

Amabilis Press
Gig Harbor, WA USA

For information, please go to facebook.com/AmabilisPress
or contact AmabilisPress@hotmail.com

For my mom,

Firefighter Mary

It is a beautiful day! Firefighter Mary gets her gear together and drives to work at the fire station. She loves to go to work, so she smiles and waves to people on her way.

When Firefighter Mary gets to the fire station she is happy to see Allen and Patrick, the firefighters she will be working with.

The last member of the crew is fire engine E-9. It has compartments to hold rescue equipment and tools to help people. It carries ladders and hoses. It also has buttons and gauges to control the water pumps.

At the start of her shift Firefighter Mary does equipment checks. She makes sure everything on the engine and all of her personal gear, such as her bunker suit and breathing apparatus, are ready to go.

The crew gets called out to help people who were in a car accident. Police Officer Howie stops traffic.

One person is injured. Firefighter Mary helps her
until the Medic Unit crew takes her to the hospital.

When they get back to the fire station, a man stops by to have his blood pressure checked. Firefighter Mary is happy to take it for him.

Then, Firefighter Mary and her crew work out. To do their best as firefighters, it is important for them to stay strong and physically fit.

After lunch, Firefighter Mary teaches a first aid and CPR class to students who come to the fire station.

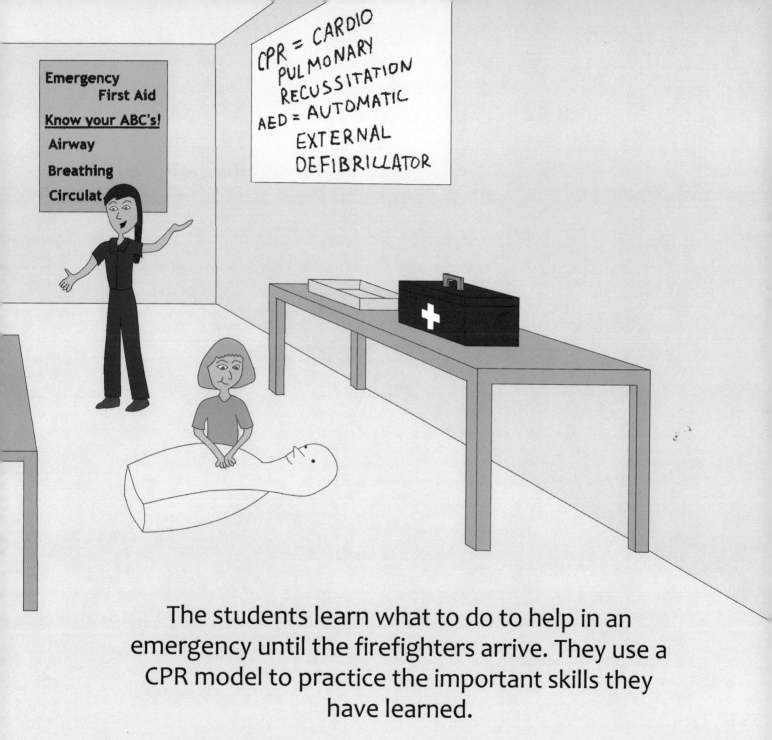

The students learn what to do to help in an emergency until the firefighters arrive. They use a CPR model to practice the important skills they have learned.

Firefighter Allen has made a big pot of delicious chili for the crew for dinner. Yum! During their meal, the alarm starts ringing loudly.

Oh no! There is an apartment building on fire! The firefighters leave their dinner and hurry to get their bunker gear on, get in the fire engine, and drive quickly to the scene of the emergency.

When the fire crew gets to the apartment building,
they make sure all the people get out safely.

Everyone left the building when they heard the smoke alarms, and they remembered to crawl so they could stay below the smoke. Firefighter Mary and her crew make sure all the people are OK.

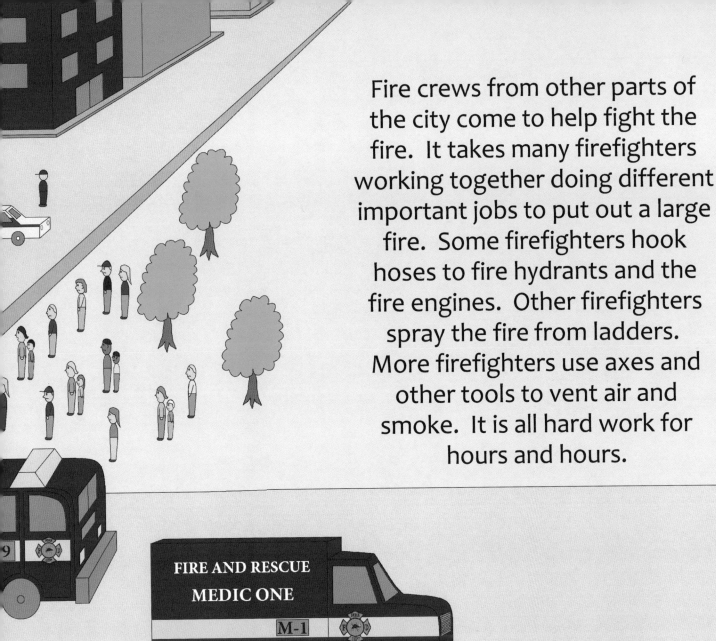

Fire crews from other parts of the city come to help fight the fire. It takes many firefighters working together doing different important jobs to put out a large fire. Some firefighters hook hoses to fire hydrants and the fire engines. Other firefighters spray the fire from ladders. More firefighters use axes and other tools to vent air and smoke. It is all hard work for hours and hours.

FIRE AND RESCUE

MEDIC ONE

M-1

Firefighter Mary and her crew go into the building and spray the fire with water from their fire hose. It is hot, smoky, and dangerous. They use their breathing apparatuses to be able to work in the smoke. Lights and reflectors help them see each other in the dark and their bunker suit protects them from the heat. Firefighters have trained for years to fight fires. They have the best equipment to do the job.

Finally, after a lot of work by all the firefighters, the fire is put out. By this time, it is very late at night.

The fire crew gets back to the fire station.
They clean up their gear and get it ready in
case they have to go to another emergency.

It has been a busy day and the crew is very tired.
They all get some sleep in the bunk room.

In the morning, the next crew gets to the fire station for their shift. Firefighter Jen, Firefighter James, and Firefighter Gina are ready for work.

Firefighter Mary, Firefighter Patrick, and Firefighter Allen are ready to go home to see their families and rest up for another work day.

When Firefighter Mary gets home, her children are very happy to see her. They miss her when she is at work, but they look forward to her coming home and telling them stories about her exciting day.

Firefighter Mary tells her kids about how she wanted to be a firefighter when she was a young girl. It took hard work and perseverance to achieve her goal. She did it and you can, too!

Made in the USA
Charleston, SC
14 May 2013